For my mother, Louise Barclay and in memory of my father, Harold Barclay.

Grateful acknowledgement and appreciation is given to the friends, associates and luminaries who contributed to this book, and who served as an inspiration to me.

Copyright© MCMLXXXIX by The C.R. Gibson Company
Text copyright© MCMLXXXIX by Dolores Barclay
All rights reserved
No part of this book may be reproduced in any form or by any means, electronic or mechanical, including photocopying, recording, or by any information storage and retrieval system without the written permission of the publisher.
Published by The C.R. Gibson Company, Norwalk, CT 06856
The photographic acknowledgements that appear on the colophon page are hereby made a part of this copyright page.
ISBN 0-8378-1874-5
GB610
Printed in the U.S.A.

Believe In Yourself

by Dolores Barclay

Ideals are like stars: you will not succeed in touching them with your hands. But like the seafaring men on the desert waters, you choose them as your guides, and following them you will reach your destiny.
Carl Schurz

Life can be a great river, branching off into paths for us to choose. Some are muddy and shallow; some are swift and dangerous; others are clear and calm.

Discovering the right path to take is not easy, and only you will know which waters flow best for you. When you finally make that decision, the pain, anguish and fear of choosing will vanish. Negative feelings will be replaced by something precious and lovely, something you can't give to anyone else nor they to you.

This wonderful blessing is called believing in yourself.

It is a celebration of you and everything you are—a celebration not guided by superficial ego but undertaken with humility and grace. God created you. He gave you goodness and talents. Others see this in you.

They enjoy your character as well as your quirks, your wisdom as well as your temperament, your strength as well as your vulnerability. They share

your sunshine and your hope, your darkness and despair. They find joy in you as you are.

You, too, can learn to embrace this joy of you.

When you learn to value yourself your soul will sing and your spirit will smile.

Offtimes nothing profits more than self-esteem.

John Milton

*Resolve to be thyself; and know that he who finds himself,
loses his misery.*

Matthew Arnold

*No man can produce great things who is not thoroughly
sincere in dealing with himself.*

Pythia

Elizabeth was ashamed of her family and herself. Her father was a day laborer and her mother worked nights as a waitress in a local diner.

She was an extremely bright young woman and won scholarships to a private school and later to a good college. But all through those school years, she never invited a friend to her home; she didn't think it was good enough.

You see, Elizabeth's family lived simply but not lavishly in a two-bedroom rented cottage in a run-down part of her hometown. There was little furniture: an old black and white TV set, a tattered sleeper couch with a plastic cover, a formica kitchen table with folding chairs and a large recliner. Away at private schools, Elizabeth stayed aloof. She avoided telling her friends exactly where she lived. She made up excuses when they invited her out to a party. She was afraid her classmates would make fun of her clothes. She knew they had been exposed to much more in life than she. Elizabeth had never seen a play; her friends talked of theaters and concerts they'd been to. Elizabeth's only travel had been from home to school; her friends had been to foreign countries.

As time went on, Elizabeth grew more and more introverted. Those who had sincerely liked her didn't want to be around her — they thought she was a snob

for not inviting them to her home or introducing them to her parents.

When Elizabeth's mother suffered a heart attack, the crisis forced Elizabeth to confront her feelings. Then she realized how much her mother had sacrificed to make Elizabeth's life a little brighter. She loved her mother yet all those years she had felt shame and disdain for her.

Elizabeth had been so self-absorbed, trying to be something other than herself, that she had lost her self-esteem.

Elizabeth is now trying to regain and honor her family's values. She's trying to share her real self with her friends. She started by showing off her clothes at school and telling her friends that her mother, a waitress, had sewn them for her.

It took a bit of courage for Elizabeth to reveal herself. But her joy is in her freedom to be all that she was created to be and to see the worth in God's gift to her — her life exactly as he gave it.

*Afoot and light-hearted I take to the open road, healthy,
free, the world before me. The long brown path before me
leading wherever I choose.* Walt Whitman

How wonderful that God's greatest gift to us, our life, should yield even more treasures by giving us the opportunity to choose our own paths, make our own decisions and realize our own individual destinies and goals. And by believing, trusting and respecting ourselves, we are put in touch with the Divine.

Yes, you can set goals. You can dare to dream. At times you may feel lost, confused, frustrated or alone. Those feeling are normal and to be expected. But you will fill yourself with even more fears if you doubt your decisions. What if I choose the wrong path? What if it doesn't work out? What if I lose everything? What if I fail? What if I'm alone?

Yes, you can make wrong turns; you can slosh through those muddy shallow waters; you can fight the rapids with all your might and still go under; you can stand forever in the clear, calm seas and not be able to see the tips of your toes.

But, remember that God gave you the gift of choice. You'll always win simply by having the courage and integrity to take that gift, seize your destiny and find your way. Your decision may not turn out to be clever or even wise, but it is right even if it only teaches you. Take heart in knowing this and be not afraid.

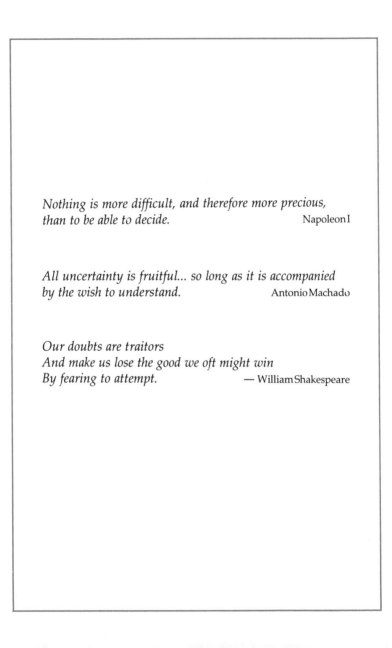

Nothing is more difficult, and therefore more precious,
than to be able to decide.   Napoleon I

All uncertainty is fruitful... so long as it is accompanied
by the wish to understand.   Antonio Machado

Our doubts are traitors
And make us lose the good we oft might win
By fearing to attempt.   — William Shakespeare

Shall I show you the muscular training of a philosopher? 'What muscles are those?' — a will undisappointed; evils avoided; powers daily exercised; careful resolutions; unerring decisions.

Epictetus

I believe very strongly that you should follow your star. It doesn't matter if you succeed as long as you make the effort.

Douglas Fairbanks, Jr.

Having choices, taking risks and making changes are the natural order of things. Before we walk, we must crawl. Before we advance to college, we must go to grade school, then junior and senior high schools. This journey to adulthood is filled with change and risk every step of the way—we just don't know it all the time because many of these choices are made for us.

I never did anything worth doing by accident, nor did any of my inventions come by accident; they came by work.

Thomas A. Edison

Rashness is the error of youth, timid cautions of age. Manhood is...the ripe and fertile season of action, when alone we can hope to find the head to contrive, united with the head to execute.

Charles Caleb Colton

All growth is a leap in the dark, a spontaneous, unpremeditated act without benefit of experience.

Henry Miller

Life is full of chances and changes, and the most prosperous of men may in the evening of his days meet with great misfortune.
Aristotle

Certainty generally is illusion, and repose is not the destiny of man.
Oliver Wendell Holmes, Jr.

The absurd man is he who never changes.

Auguste Bathelemy

We accept the verdict of the past until the need for changes cries out loudly enough to force upon us a choice between the comforts of further inertia and the irksomeness of action.

Learned Hand

Without risk, you don't experience life. Life is like a road. There are all kinds of ways. If you go straight, you'll never see what's behind that other road. If you don't take a right or left, you'll never experience everything that's there.

Frederique van der Wal

Begin by asking yourself what you truly want, not what others expect or demand of you. Once you know, hold on to that vision and set your goal. Then examine all the paths before you: What makes one better than another? What makes one worse than another?

There are no set rules for setting goals and reaching them. The process is as individual and creative, and often as frustrating, as all the daily chores we begrudgingly perform, such as picking clothes to wear or paying the bills.

Life was meant to be lived, and curiousity must be kept alive. One must never, for whatever reason, turn his back on life. Eleanor Roosevelt

The shoe that fits one person pinches another; there is no recipe for living that suits all cases. Carl Jung

Be absolutely clear what it is you want. Cast aside
all other considerations and distractions. Your goal
is most important and should come first. Then, stick
to your goal—no matter what setbacks or frustrations
you may encounter.

If you want to be organized about goal-setting, start
at the beginning. Sit down in a quiet place so that
you can be alone with your thoughts. Take a deep
breath and picture or imagine your goal. See it as a
finished product, a reality. Feel its texture, see its
color and hear its pulse. You can bring your goal to
life.

Try working toward your goal one day at a time. Accept little advances. Study them to make sure they're strong enough to support the next step and that they are pointing in the right direction. Examine setbacks and consider how you can turn them to your advantage.

Inch along. Don't lose sight of your quest. You are creating a solid foundation from which you will eventually reach your goal.

I speak without exaggeration when I say I have con-structed three thousand different theories in connection with the electric light.   Yet in only two cases did my experiments prove the truth of my theory.

Thomas A. Edison

Once you reach your goal, nurture it. Respect it and appreciate what you have accomplished. And don't be surprised if you are suddenly faced with yet new choices!

If what I want to accomplish seems monumental I am overwhelmed. I've found that looking at it as a series of smaller tasks helps me. Then I'm to work toward my goal without fear or hesitation. Barbara Hill-Goullet

There is no use whatever trying to help people who do not help themselves. You cannot push anyone up a ladder unless he is willing to climb himself.

Andrew Carnegie

And so you give birth to another adventure. But now, you have some experience and a little wisdom. Are you apprehensive? Remember how strong you are and how much stronger you're becoming. Observe how much you've grown and what you've learned. No one can ever take that experience away from you. You own that.

Your experiences will open doors to new challenges and goals. Don't view this unveiling as a chore, a drudge or a problem. See it as a revelation of possibilities: a baptism in vitality.
Breathe deeply, drinking the treasures of life.

As you move forward, don't set yourself against others: Compare your progress only to yourself and your dreams. Goals are as individual as fingerprints.

End the day and be done with it. You have achieved what you could. If blunders occurred; forget them. Tomorrow is a new day, begin it well and serenely and with a spirit too high to be encumbered with nonsense.

This day is too dear, with it's hopes and invitations, to waste a moment on the yesterdays.

Ralph Waldo Emerson

Perfection is an ideal. Set expectations in line with your abilities, and just see what you can accomplish!

Dr. Dana Luck

Seek the truth of what you are doing and seek understanding. God is with you. Those who love and cherish you are with you. And, you have a worthy companion in yourself.

So take a deep breath, pick yourself up, dust yourself off and let your soul begin to hum its song.

Welcome, O life! I go to encounter for the millionth time the reality of experience.

James Joyce

Colophon

Designed by Bob Pantelone
Typeset in Palatino

Photographs:
Four By Five pp. 6, 7; Joseph Di Chello pp. 8, 16,
21, 24; Jim Patrick pp. 11, 15; Three Lions pg. 12;
Nance Trueworthy pp. 13, 14, 22, 23; Marie
Demarest pg. 17; Photo Resources pp. 19, 25, 27,
30, 31, 34; Roger Smith pg. 20; Leslie Irvin pg.
28; Ken Blumberg pg. 32; Peter Haynes pg. 33.